Charles Dickens

HARD TIMES

Sweet Cherry

THE Charles Dickens

CHILDREN'S COLLECTION

Published by Sweet Cherry Publishing Limited
Unit 36, Vulcan House,
Vulcan Road,
Leicester, LE5 3EF
United Kingdom

First published in the UK in 2020
2020 edition

2 4 6 8 10 9 7 5 3

ISBN: 978-1-78226-486-6

Charles Dickens: Hard Times

Based on the original story from Charles Dickens,
adapted by Philip Gooden.

Cover design by Pipi Sposito and Margot Reverdiau
Illustrations by Maria Lia Malandrino

Lexile® code numerical measure L = Lexile® 630L

Guided Reading Level = Q

www.sweetcherrypublishing.com

Printed and bound in Turkey
T.IO006

GRUMPY OLD GRADGRIND

A long time ago, in the middle of England, there was a dull, dusty town called Coketown. It was full of factories: huge, looming, red-brick factories with hundreds of windows

that watched over the town like the eyes of giants.

The streets where the townspeople lived were very similar to each other. And the lives of the townspeople were very similar too. Every day they woke up at the same time, ate the same measly breakfast and went to work in the same sooty factories.

As you can imagine, life in Coketown was very dull and very boring. Except that, in Coketown, you couldn't *imagine* anything. There was no space for imagination. The only things that mattered in Coketown were cold, hard facts. Facts and figures and money, of course. Money mattered.

Mr Thomas Gradgrind ran a school near Coketown. He too was only interested in facts, figures and money.

Everything about Mr Gradgrind was straight or square. He had a solid, square forehead and straight, dark eyebrows that cast a permanent shadow over his eyes.

At this moment, Mr Gradgrind's square-tipped finger was pointing towards a young girl.

'Who is that girl?' he snapped, his mouth twisting into a frown.

'I'm Sissy Jupe, sir,' the girl said.

'Sissy is not a name,' said Mr Gradgrind. 'Do not call yourself Sissy. Call yourself Cecilia.'

'It is my father who calls me Sissy, sir,' she explained in a trembling voice.

'Then he must stop doing that,' said Mr Gradgrind. 'Tell him that he must never call you Sissy again. What does your father do?'

'He – he works in a circus, sir.'

Judging by the expression on Mr Gradgrind's face, it was clear that he did not approve of the circus.

'My father works with horses,' said Sissy.

'Is that so? Tell me, *Cecilia*, what is your definition of a horse?' asked Mr Gradgrind.

Sissy Jupe looked confused. A horse is a horse – how else could you define it? Sissy said nothing. Her face turned a deep shade of red.

'The girl is unable to define a horse!' said Mr Gradgrind. 'Which *boy* can tell me what a horse is? How about you, Bitzer?'

The boy called Bitzer had very fair hair and freckles.

'A quadruped,' he said. Meaning that a horse has four legs.

'Graminivorous,' he said. Meaning that a horse eats grass.

'A horse has forty teeth and hard hooves. Though hard, horse's hooves are also given iron shoes.'

Bitzer said a lot more. At each point Mr Gradgrind nodded his head in approval.

'Very well,' he said, smiling and folding his arms. 'That is a horse. Now, let me ask, girls and boys.

Would you decorate your bedrooms with pictures of horses? What about with wallpaper covered with pictures of horses?'

Half the class shouted, 'Yes, sir!'

Seeing that this was the wrong answer, the other half shouted, 'No, sir!'

'Of course you would not. And why not?'

Silence. No one knew the answer.

'I'll explain, then,' said Mr Gradgrind. 'Do you ever see horses walking up and down walls in real life? Do you?'

'No, sir!' said the class.

'Of course you do not,' said Mr Gradgrind. 'Horses do not walk up walls. So then, why on earth would you cover you walls with pictures of horses? It is ridiculous! You should not see things that aren't real. Forget such silly things as imagination. Forget myths, forget magic, forget fairy tales. Facts are everything!'

Mr Gradgrind walked away from the school feeling rather pleased with himself. He may have even had a spring in his step if he approved of such things, which, of course, he did not. So he walked at his usual pace, with his usual serious expression.

Mr Gradgrind's good mood
lasted until he reached the border
of Coketown. There, he paused and
looked around. He was sure that he
heard the tinkling of joyful music
floating on the wind. And he was

quite certain that he saw a scattering
of colourful wooden caravans.

And, good heavens! There was an
obnoxiously large, striped tent. The
flag flying above it read: *SLEARY'S
CIRCUS*.

Mr Gradgrind's straight line of a mouth turned once again into a frown. Circuses were colourful and fun – the exact opposite of Coketown. What sort of example would this silly show set his students? The moment they saw a galloping horse, juggling clown or leotard-wearing tightrope walker, they would forget all about the importance of facts and figures. They would want to have *fun*.

Already, children were crouching by a gap in the tent curtains, taking turns to peer at the performers inside.

These could not possibly be students from *his* school.

Mr Gradgrind took his glasses from his pocket and perched them on the end of his nose. What he saw did not please him. Among the

curious children were his daughter, Louisa, and his son, Tom. Louisa was sixteen and Tom was a year younger.

Mr Gradgrind grabbed hold of his son and daughter and started leading them away.

'What on earth are you doing here?' he barked.

'I wanted to see what it was like,' said Louisa. 'The circus is leaving soon and I just *had* to see it.'

'What would your friends say, Louisa?' her father tutted. 'What would Mr Bounderby say?'

As soon as Mr Bounderby's name had left her father's mouth, Louisa's face transformed. Her eyes narrowed, her eyebrows crinkled, and her lips were so firmly pressed together that it would have been impossible for her to answer her father's question.

MEET MR BOUNDERBY

Mr Bounderby was a very large man and a very rich one, too. He owned three factories and a bank, called Bounderby's Bank.

Perhaps because of his wealth, or perhaps it was simply his personality, Mr Josiah Bounderby thought that he was the most important man in the world.

Standing in the best room in Stone Lodge (the home of the Gradgrinds), next to Mrs Gradgrind (a small, thin woman, who was often ill), Mr Bounderby looked like a giant.

He was boasting in a loud voice
to Mrs Gradgrind about something
rather unusual. Not about how rich
and powerful he was now, but about
how poor and deprived he had been
as a child.

'I did not have any shoes to cover
my little feet,' said Mr Bounderby. 'I
spent the day of my tenth birthday in
a ditch, and the night in a pigsty.

Not that a ditch was new to me, for I
was born in a ditch.'

Mrs Gradgrind gasped. She said
in a feeble voice, 'I hope it was at
least a dry ditch.'

'No!' cried Mr Bounderby. 'It had
a foot of water in it.'

'But what about your mother?' asked Mrs Gradgrind.

'My mother left me to my grandmother,' said Mr Bounderby. 'My grandmother was the wickedest old woman that ever lived. If I got a pair of shoes by any chance, she would take them off me, sell them and keep the money for herself!'

He went on to boast of how, after this terrible start in life, he had worked his way up in the world. Now look at him – the owner of three factories and a bank.

At this moment, Mr Gradgrind arrived home with Tom and Louisa. If Mr Gradgrind had one friend in the world, it was Mr Bounderby. And if Mr Bounderby had one friend in the world, it was Mr Gradgrind. But neither man believed in friendship. It wasn't a fact, you see. It wasn't a figure. It couldn't be measured, so to them it did not exist.

The two men talked about the *fact* that a girl at school, Sissy Jupe, was the daughter of a circus performer.

Mr Bounderby said she should be thrown out of the school. He said that he and Mr Gradgrind should go that instant to see her father and tell him that Sissy was no longer welcome due to her connection with the circus.

As they left Stone Lodge, Mr Bounderby called to Louisa, 'Goodbye, dearest Louisa!'

'Goodbye, Mr Bounderby,' Louisa replied coldly. Louisa knew that she was Mr Bounderby's favourite. She hated that fact and, deep down, she hated Mr Bounderby too.

When Mr Bounderby and Mr
Gradgrind reached the circus,
they found the tents folded away

and the signs taken down. The circus was leaving Coketown. That was good.

What was not good, however, was that Sissy Jupe's father had left already. He had deserted both Sissy and the circus, and no one knew why. Sissy was scared and sad and all alone.

Mr Gradgrind walked over to where Sissy was sitting, tears raining down her flushed cheeks.

'I'll make you an offer,' Mr Gradgrind said, quite out of the blue. 'You can leave today with the circus, or you can come to live at Stone Lodge with my family. My wife is very sick, she could do with someone to look after her. You can do that and continue your education.'

Sissy was shocked. Mr Gradgrind had never showed kindness like this to anyone. Without much time to think, Sissy agreed. She packed

a very small bag and left, waving
goodbye to her circus family.

THE START OF SISSY AND LOUISA

Louisa Gradgrind was very close to her brother, Tom. They both grew up within the bare, boring walls of Stone Lodge, both wishing for music, poetry and paintings – things they were not allowed.

Once, as a child, Louisa had turned to her brother and said, 'Tom, I wonder–' But, before she could finish her sentence, Mr Gradgrind bellowed, 'Louisa, never wonder!

Wondering leads to imagining and imagination is not good for anything.'

From that moment on, Louisa never wondered. She never dreamed or imagined, and soon enough, she even found it difficult to feel things. She was never happy or sad, she was just *there*.

Tom, meanwhile, grew into a sulky, angry young man.

One day, Tom said to Louisa: 'I wish I could collect all the facts and figures we hear so much about, and all the people who discovered them. I wish I could put a thousand barrels of gunpowder under them and blow them all up!'

He may not have liked facts and figures, but Louisa's brother was soon going to start work in Mr Bounderby's bank. Facts and figures were things he would have to get used to.

Sissy Jupe had not been raised in the same way as the Gradgrind children. At first, she did not enjoy living with them. She would sit awake at night, tears blurring her eyes as she thought over and over about running away. She wanted to leave this sad, boring town and go back to the circus and her father. But she could not bear to, because her father was not with the circus anymore. She could leave for somewhere else, anywhere else … but what if, one day, he came back for her and she was not in Coketown anymore? No, she could not risk it. She would have to stay.

Over time, however, Sissy did settle into life at Stone Lodge. She started to look up to Louisa. She thought Louisa was very smart – a lot smarter than people gave her credit for.

The two girls were very different from one another. Sissy was kind-hearted and fun, and tried to always be positive, while Louisa was distant and cold. She focused only on facts and never saw much to be positive about. But though different, Sissy and Louisa grew very close. Eventually, it felt as if they were more like sisters than friends.

Sissy would tell Louisa stories about her father. She said that he was the circus's funniest clown. That he used to do gravity-defying tricks on horseback and make up hilarious routines with his performing dog, Merrylegs.

But with each passing year, he had got older and weaker. His tricks hadn't worked as well as they once had, and he had often injured himself.

One day, as the circus was preparing to leave town, Sissy's father had sent her out to buy some healing oil for his bumps and bruises. When she returned, her father had left and taken Merrylegs with him. That was the day that Mr Gradgrind invited Sissy to live at Stone Lodge. And though she was happy now, she

still kept the bottle of healing oil.
She thought that her father might
need it one day, when he came back.

The Mysterious Old Woman

On a cool autumn afternoon,
Tom Gradgrind went to visit
Mr Bounderby. They sat in Mr
Bounderby's dim, grey drawing
room, drank weak tea and talked
endlessly about the boring work that
Tom was going to do at Bounderby's
Bank.

Tom did not like the sound of his
new job. But he found that he only
had to say 'Louisa would like this'

or 'Louisa wouldn't like that' for Mr Bounderby to change his mind about which tasks Tom would have to do. Louisa was his *favourite*, so whatever Louisa would like would happen.

Just as Tom was walking down the stone steps from Mr Bounderby's front door, he felt something touch his arm. It was the hand of an old woman.

She was tall and simply dressed. Her shoes were muddy and tattered, as if she had walked a long way. She carried a large umbrella and a little basket.

'Sir, if you please,' she said. 'Have you seen the gentleman who lives there?'

She pointed her umbrella up to Mr Bounderby's front door.

Tom nodded.

'And how did he look, sir?' the old woman asked. 'Was he well and cheerful?'

Tom thought of the man he had

just left. Did Mr Bounderby
ever look well or cheerful?
Not really. But the woman
looked worried, so Tom said
to her, 'Yes, he is well and
cheerful.'

'Oh, thank you, sir,
thank you! I have walked

miles today to find that out. I am so pleased to finally hear the answer.'

Tom walked off, leaving the old woman staring at the large square house in wonder. He was curious about the woman's strange behaviour. Why would she walk miles simply to ask if a grumpy old factory owner was well?

A NOT-SO-WONDERFUL WEDDING

A few years went by with no sign of the strange old woman.

Mr Gradgrind continued to run his school, teaching the children about facts and figures.

Mr Bounderby grew richer and richer, thanks to his bank. The bank that poor Tom Gradgrind now worked at.

And Louisa Gradgrind?

Louisa's life changed on the day

her father called her into his study
at Stone Lodge. 'Louisa,' he said,
very seriously. 'I have just had a very
important talk with a very important
man. A man who would like to
marry you.'

Louisa's face fell. Her breath caught in her throat. She had a horrible feeling that she knew which man her father was talking about.

Mr Gradgrind continued: 'Mr Bounderby has asked me for your hand in marriage.'

'Father,' said Louisa, 'do you think I love Mr Bounderby?'

Mr Gradgrind looked like he had bitten into a large lemon. 'Let us stick to the facts, Louisa,' he said. 'Does Mr Bounderby want to marry you? Yes, he does. That is a fact.

The only question you have to answer is: should you marry him?'

'And should I marry him?' asked Louisa, staring at her father.

'I – I can't answer that. It has to be you who decides.'

'Mr Bounderby is much older than I am.'

'Yes, he is.'

Louisa stood up and walked over to the window. She peered out at the smoking chimneys of Coketown.

'I will accept Mr Bounderby's proposal,' she said, finally.

'A wise decision, my dear,' said

her father. He sounded relieved. As Louisa shut the door to her father's study, she felt a heavy weight drop in her stomach. She felt sick. Hot, salty tears spilt from her eyes.

'Mr Bounderby is very rich,'
she whispered to herself. 'He has
factories and a bank. Marrying him is
a wise decision. I am doing the right
thing.' But the facts did not make her
feel any better.

Louisa Gradgrind and Mr
Bounderby were married eight
weeks later, in a plain grey church in
Coketown.

Tom was pleased that his sister
was marrying Mr Bounderby. Tom
was greedy. He thought that he could
use his sister's miserable marriage

to get extra money out of Mr
Bounderby.

In fact, the only person who was
sad about Louisa leaving Stone
Lodge was Sissy Jupe. She knew that
Louisa did not love Mr Bounderby.
But Sissy did not say anything.

A Very Small Robbery

The very moment that Louisa returned from her dreadfully dreary honeymoon with Mr Bounderby, she heard a knock at the door.

'Louisa!' Tom cried as he walked into the large, square hallway of Mr Bounderby's house. 'I hope that you had a wonderful trip. I don't suppose you have a moment of time for your dear brother?'

Tom smiled wickedly at his sister's confused face. 'You see, I'm in a spot of bother and I could really use your help. I have lost a little money through gambling. Well, a lot of money, really. I was hoping that you could lend me a few pounds to pay my debts.'

Louisa gave her brother as much money as she could. She loved her brother – it was one of the few emotions she was sure of. And Tom, in his own selfish way, loved his sister, too.

But Louisa's money soon ran out, and the people whom Tom owed money to were becoming less patient and more angry with each passing day. Tom's money worries were making him ill. Soon he was pale and thin, and looked much older than his years.

༉༄

More time passed and things moved steadily on. Until, one warm summer's evening, when the factories had shut for the night and the town lay in a sleepy silence, something shocking happened.

'Someone has broken into the bank!' The cry rose throughout the streets until it reached Mr Bounderby's ears.

One hundred and fifty pounds was stolen. Someone had made a copy of the key to the safe. Then, in the middle of the night, they had broken into the bank, tiptoed down the cold, stone halls, opened the safe with the copied key and stolen the money.

Mr Bounderby was raging. He marched off to the bank the moment he heard the news. When he returned home to find that his wife

had left him, he was angrier still. Louisa had returned to Stone Lodge and her family.

Louisa explained to her father that she and her husband had nothing in common. He was old: she was young. He was only interested in making money: she was not. And they did not love each other. These were facts.

'I wish it were different,' Louisa said, finally, 'but it isn't different and so … and so …' But Louisa could not finish what she was saying. She fell to the floor in tears.

For only the second time in his life, Mr Gradgrind was touched not by facts, but by feelings.

He gently lifted Louisa up from where she was lying and wrapped his arms around her until, at last, she stopped crying. Then Mr Gradgrind sent for Sissy Jupe, who still lived at Stone Lodge. He asked Sissy to look after his daughter.

Sissy was happy to help. She had missed Louisa. The two women talked together, walked together and soon felt almost like sisters again. Louisa's heart, once hardened with facts and figures, was starting to soften.

Mr Gradgrind was changing too. Eventually, he decided to go with his wife to see Mr Bounderby. He was planning to tell his friend that Louisa would not be returning. She would be staying with her family at Stone Lodge.

THE TRUTH ABOUT MR BOUNDERBY

While Louisa was settling herself
back into life at Stone Lodge,
the investigation into the theft at
Bounderby's Bank continued.

A strange old woman had been
spotted outside places belonging
to Mr Bounderby. Outside his
house, his factories, his bank.
She carried a large umbrella
and a small basket. It was the
same mysterious woman who

had spoken to Tom Gradgrind that autumn afternoon.

Thinking that she must be the thief, the police arrested her and took her to Mr Bounderby's house.

The mysterious lady was not the only guest at Mr Bounderby's home that afternoon. The heavy knock on the front door sounded just as Mr and Mrs Gradgrind and Tom sat down in Mr Bounderby's drawing room.

A servant showed the policeman and the frightened old woman into the drab drawing room.

'Mr Bounderby, sir,' the policeman said. 'Here is the person you have been looking for. This lady robbed your bank.'

Mr Bounderby's face turned white with shock. His eyes opened wide and his eyebrows raised themselves to sit so far up his forehead that they looked as if they may never come back down.

'It was not easy to find this crook, Mr Bounderby,' said the policeman. 'But it is always a pleasure to help you.'

'W-w-why did you bring her here?' Mr Bounderby stuttered.

'My dear Josiah!' cried the old woman. 'My darling boy!'

The policeman and the Gradgrinds looked from the old woman to Mr Bounderby and back again in surprise. What was going on?

'I did as you said, Josiah,' said the woman. 'I never told anyone that I was your mother. I just came to

Coketown from time to time to take a peep at you and your fine house, and your factory and your bank. It was a proud peep.'

Now Mr Gradgrind stepped forwards.

'How dare you,' he said to the woman. 'If you are Mr Bounderby's mother, then you are the woman who deserted him when he was a baby. You left him to his awful grandmother to look after.

Mr Bounderby spent his tenth birthday in a ditch!'

'Deserted my dear Josiah? Never! His father died when Josiah was eight, but I scrimped and saved to make sure Josiah never went without. He was given the best I could afford. I would never have left him.'

Mr Bounderby's face turned from white to red. The truth had finally come out. He had not been born in a ditch or abandoned by his mother. He was a liar!

The shocking news soon spread through Coketown.

Mr Bounderby's face, once swelled with pride, now sat slumped against his chest like a popped balloon.

BACK TO
SLEARY'S CIRCUS

The police were baffled. If the strange old woman had not robbed Mr Bounderby's bank, then who had?

If only the people in Mr Bounderby's drawing room that afternoon had turned their heads just slightly, they might have known. They might have noticed how uncomfortable Tom Gradgrind seemed – particularly when the policeman mentioned the bank robbery. For the truth was that it was Tom himself who had robbed his employer's bank. He needed the money to pay his gambling debts.

Each time someone mentioned the crime, Tom's cheeks flushed and his heart began to beat faster. He was convinced that he was going to be found out. He had to tell someone, but he could not turn to Louisa. He could not bear to see the look of shame on his sister's face. Instead, he turned to Sissy Jupe.

'Where can I go?' he asked. 'I'm sure the police will work out that I'm guilty if I stay here. But I have very little money and no friends to hide me!'

Sissy thought for a moment.

'My father's old circus,' she said.

'Sleary's Circus. They travel to Liverpool at this time of year. Go to Liverpool and tell the circus that I sent you. They will keep you safe.'

Tom did as Sissy told him.

When Louisa discovered Tom's crime, she was horrified. Mr Gradgrind was shocked and angry at Tom, and at Sissy for keeping it a secret. But he had changed. The pity and love he felt for both of them were stronger than his anger.

Mr Gradgrind and Louisa asked Sissy to take them to Liverpool, to Sleary's Circus.

The circus was just as Sissy remembered: full of colour, light, movement and laughter. It had everything that Coketown did not.

Within the brightly striped tent, they found Tom. He was working as a clown – making people smile and laugh, and joking with the other performers; things he had never been able to do before. Mr

Gradgrind's heart sank a little when he saw his son's smiling face. He felt guilty for making his children's lives so dull and dreary. And though he could see that Tom was enjoying the circus, he knew what had to be done.

Mr Gradgrind arranged to sneak Tom on board a ship sailing from Liverpool to America. He, Sissy and Louisa tearfully said goodbye to Tom.

Tom, however, didn't feel sad when
he waved goodbye to his family. He
didn't shed a single tear. It was not
until he reached America and realised
that he would never see them again,
that he finally started to miss them.

Once they had bid farewell to Tom,
Mr Gradgrind asked Mr Sleary whether
he had any news of Louisa's father.

'Oh dear,' said Mr Sleary. 'You
didn't know? Merrylegs came back by
himself. That dog would never have
deserted his master, not as long as
he was alive. I'm afraid that old Jupe
must be dead.'

Mr Gradgrind turned away. Tears stung his eyes, but he said nothing. His heart was too full.

❧

Time moved on, as did the Gradgrind family.

Mr Gradgrind no longer lived by facts and figures.

Sissy married and had children. Though she never stopped missing her father, the memories of him now made her smile rather than cry.

Louisa did not marry again, after Mr Bounderby. Instead, she devoted herself to Sissy's children, becoming

like a second mother to them. And to
Sissy she was, and always would be,
a sister.

Charles Dickens

Charles Dickens was born in Portsmouth in 1812. Like many of the characters he wrote about, his family were poor and his childhood was difficult. As an adult, he became known around the world for his books. He is remembered as one of the most important writers of his time.

To download Charles Dickens activities, please visit
www.sweetcherrypublishing.com/resources